I0643764

wild canines

JACKALS

David Lee

PowerKiDS press.
New York

Published in 2017 by The Rosen Publishing Group, Inc.
29 East 21st Street, New York, NY 10010

First Edition

Editor: Caitie McAneney
Book Design: Tanya Dellaccio

Photo Credits: Cover EcoPrint/Shutterstock.com; cover, pp. 3–6, 8, 10–12, 14–16, 18–20, 22–24 (background) lliveinoctober/Shutterstock.com; p. 4 francesco de marco/Shutterstock.com; p. 5 (Ethiopian wolf) ArCaLu/Shutterstock.com; p. 5 (African wild dog) sivanadar/Shutterstock.com; p. 5 (jackal) JONATHAN PLEDGER/Shutterstock.com; p. 6 (golden jackal) Dr Ajay Kumar Singh/Shutterstock.com; p. 6 (side-striped jackal) Chris Fourle/Shutterstock.com; p. 7 romas photo/Shutterstock.com; p. 9 Paul Lathbury/Lathersp ics/Getty Images; p. 11 (top) Bildagentur Zoonar GmbH/Shutterstock.com; p. 11 (bottom) Four Oaks/Shutterstock.com; p. 13 Albie Venter/Shutterstock.com; p. 15 (top) Bryan Busovicki/Shutterstock.com; p. 15 (bottom) john michael evan potter/Shutterstock.com; p. 17 Gerhard Strydom/Shutterstock.com; p. 19 (top) Travel Stock/Shutterstock.com; p. 19 (bottom) Stacey Ann Alberts/Shutterstock.com; p. 21 Sumit Chakraborty Photography/Getty Images; p. 22 paula french/Shutterstock.com.

Cataloging-in-Publication Data

Names: Lee, David.
Title: Jackals / David Lee.
Description: New York : PowerKids Press, 2017. | Series: Wild canines | Includes index.
Identifiers: ISBN 9781499420272 (pbk.) | ISBN 9781499420296 (library bound) | ISBN 9781499420289 (6 pack)
Subjects: LCSH: Jackals–Juvenile literature.
Classification: LCC QL737.C22 L44 2017 | DDC 599.77'2–d23

Manufactured in the United States of America

CPSIA Compliance Information: Batch #BS16PK: For Further Information contact Rosen Publishing, New York, New York at 1-800-237-9932

CONTENTS

The Clever Jackal

Jackals are wild canines that roam the deserts and grasslands of the **Eastern Hemisphere**. These wild dogs are smaller than other animals in the canine family, such as wolves and dingoes.

Throughout history, many groups of people have thought of jackals as clever and sneaky. They even created **folklore** about these canines. This might have something to do with jackals' nighttime **scavenging**. Thousands of years ago, the Egyptians believed in a god named Anubis who was part jackal. Anubis guided the dead to the underworld.

That's Wild!
This Egyptian artwork shows jackal-headed Anubis leading a person who has died to be judged in the afterlife.

Many jackals live in Africa. Other wild canines that live in Africa include the African wild dog and the Ethiopian wolf.

Jackal Features

Jackals have a thin body and big, pointed ears. Most have a bushy tail. They look a bit like coyotes, which are found in North America. They weigh up to 35 pounds (15.9 kg).

There are three jackal species, or kinds. The golden jackal—also called the common jackal—is sand-colored. It's shorter than other jackal species. The side-striped jackal has stripes along the sides of its body and a white tip on its tail. Black-backed jackals are sand-colored with a black back.

golden jackal

side-striped jackal

Most people recognize the black-backed jackal because it can be more active during the day. The golden jackal and side-striped jackal are nocturnal, or most active at night.

Where to Find a Jackal

Jackals live in many kinds of **habitats** in Africa, the Middle East, southeastern Europe, India, and Southeast Asia. They **adapt** well to different temperatures and **terrains**.

Different species prefer to live in different habitats. Golden jackals are usually found in open, grassy plains and deserts from northern Africa to Southeast Asia and Europe. Black-backed jackals are found in **savannas** and woodlands in southern Africa. Side-striped jackals would rather live in wetter places, such as marshes and areas with many green plants in central and southern Africa.

That's Wild!

Some jackals also live in the mountains.

Golden jackals have the widest range of all jackal species. That means they're spread out across a great area of space.

A Pack of Jackals

Some jackals like to live and hunt alone, while others do so in pairs. However, like many canines, jackals often belong to packs. These packs are strong family units that help their members survive, find food, and raise young.

Packs usually include a male, female, and their offspring, or young. Jackal couples often mate for life, which means they make babies only with each other. The pack sometimes includes older offspring that help care for their younger brothers and sisters.

That's Wild!

Jackal packs are very **territorial**. They mark their territory with their waste.

Jackal mates make a great team when it comes to raising their pups.

Jackal Pups

A mother jackal usually gives birth to a litter of about two to six pups. Jackals give birth in dens, which can be holes in the ground. Pups are blind and unable to care for themselves when they're born. The mother jackal stays with her pups all day long.

Jackals might change dens every couple of weeks so predators can't find them. Parents bring their pups food for the first few months. Then, they teach the pups how to hunt on their own.

That's Wild!

Pups get a lot of attention and help from their older brothers and sisters!

Jackal pups love to play!

What's on the Menu?

Jackals will eat nearly anything they can find. A jackal that hunts on its own might eat small animals, such as bugs, birds, reptiles, and small **mammals**. A jackal pack might be able to hunt sheep, antelopes, or even gazelles.

When jackals aren't hunting, they eat fruits and grasses. They're also scavengers, so they'll eat dead animals left behind by large predators and trash left behind by people. Jackals have been known to hunt livestock, or farm animals, too.

That's Wild!

Sometimes a jackal will lead a large predator to its **prey**. That way, the predator will kill the animal, and the jackal can eat what's left of it.

This jackal is sharing the remains of a wildebeest with vultures, which are also scavengers.

Jackals on the Hunt

Jackals are ready to hunt when they're only six months old. Golden jackals and side-striped jackals like to hunt at night. That's when it's cooler outside and fewer predators are out.

Jackals that hunt alone may ambush their prey, or attack it by surprise. They may kill a smaller animal by biting it in the neck or shaking it. Jackals in a pack might howl to alert their pack when prey is nearby. Packs may target a large animal and attack together.

Jackals have a thin body and long legs to help them chase prey.

That's Wild!
Jackals' sharp, curved teeth help them kill their prey and eat the meat.

Surviving in the Wild

Jackals have special senses and adaptations that help them survive and hunt successfully. Jackals have an amazing sense of sight, even in the dark. That helps with nighttime hunts! They also have a great sense of hearing, thanks to their big ears. A jackal's sense of smell is possibly 100 times stronger than a person's!

A jackal's body is perfectly built for roaming long distances and chasing prey. Its sand-colored fur blends in with the dusty desert and dry grasslands. This is called camouflage.

That's Wild!

Animals that are a mixture of jackals and dogs are used to sniff for **bombs** at airports in Russia. That's because jackals have a great sense of smell!

Jackals are able to walk many miles a day to find food. Finding water is also very important for survival, especially in the desert.

Jackals at Risk

Some wild canines, such as wolves and dingoes, have no natural predators. However, the jackal has to watch out for larger predators, such as hyenas and leopards. Eagles sometimes snatch jackal pups from the ground.

However, people are the greatest danger to jackals. People have been moving onto the lands where jackals live. Roads and buildings now stand where jackals used to roam. Their territory is also used for farms. If a jackal enters a farm for a meal, it may be shot or poisoned.

That's Wild!

One way to save jackals is to create special fences, called bomas, around livestock. Then jackals can't get in and may no longer be seen as pests.

Jackals don't often attack people, but there have been some serious jackal attacks. Jackals can be deadly, especially if they have **rabies**.

One-of-a-Kind Canine

Jackals have been an important part of folklore for many different groups of people who live in their range. Jackals are also important parts of their habitats because they keep populations of small animals from growing. Luckily, this amazing hunter and scavenger isn't endangered, or at risk of dying out, any time soon.

Jackals need help to survive as people continue to build on their land. Hopefully, **conservation** efforts can save the jackals' habitat so this one-of-a-kind canine can hunt in peace for many years to come!

Glossary

adapt: To change in order to live better in a certain environment.

bomb: A device that blows up under certain conditions.

conservation: Efforts to care for the natural world.

Eastern Hemisphere: Half of Earth that contains Africa, Asia, Europe, and Australia.

folklore: Ideas or stories that may not be true but that many people have heard or read.

habitat: The natural home for plants, animals, and other living things.

mammal: A warm-blooded animal that has a backbone and hair, breathes air, and feeds milk to its young.

prey: An animal hunted by other animals for food.

rabies: A deadly disease that affects the brain, spinal cord, and nerves. It is carried in the spit of some animals.

savanna: A grassland with scattered patches of trees.

scavenge: To search for trash or dead animals to eat.

terrain: A type of land in an area.

territorial: Used to describe animals that try to keep others away from an area they use or control.

Index

Websites

Due to the changing nature of Internet links, PowerKids Press has developed an online list of websites related to the subject of this book. This site is updated regularly. Please use this link to access the list:
www.powerkidslinks.com/canine/jack